ISBN 1 85854 684 2

Copyright by The National Trust for Places of Historical Interest or Natural Beauty.
© Brimax Books Ltd 1998. All rights reserved.
Published by Brimax Books Ltd, Newmarket, England, CB8 7AU, 1998.
Printed in Spain.

The Jungle Book

By Rudyard Kipling
Adapted by Lucy Kincaid
Illustrated by Gill Guile

Brimax · Newmarket · England

The Jungle Book

One day, a baby boy finds his way into a wolf family's cave. Mother and Father Wolf decide to look after him as if he were one of their own cubs. Mother Wolf calls the little boy Mowgli.

As Mowgli grows up, he learns all there is to know about the Jungle from Baloo the bear and Bagheera the black panther. He loves his Jungle home and he makes friends with all the animals - except for Shere Khan the tiger, who becomes a dangerous enemy.

Contents

Mowgli's Brothers

Father Wolf had just woken up. It was time for him to leave his family and go hunting.

Down in the valley Shere Khan the tiger was hunting too. Father Wolf and Mother Wolf could hear him purring. Then he gave a howl.

"He's missed!" said Father Wolf.

"Something is coming," said Mother Wolf, twitching an ear. "Get ready to pounce."

The bushes rustled. Father Wolf got ready to leap, but then he stopped.

"It's a man-cub!" he said to Mother Wolf.

In front of them stood a naked, brown baby, who could barely walk. He looked at Father Wolf and laughed.

Father Wolf gently lifted the baby and put him with his own four cubs, which were snuggled up to Mother Wolf. Suddenly Shere Khan's head blocked the sunlight from the cave.

"Give the man-cub to me," said Shere Khan.

"He is ours," said Father Wolf.

"It is Shere Khan who speaks!" roared the tiger.

Mother Wolf sprang forward. "The **cub is mine!**" she snarled.

Shere Khan might have faced Father Wolf, but he did not dare face Mother Wolf. He backed off with a growl.

Mother Wolf named the baby Mowgli.

"Lie still, little Mowgli," she said. "The time will come when you will hunt Shere Khan as he has hunted you!"

The Law of the Jungle says that as soon as cubs are old enough, they must be brought before the Wolf Pack leader.

A wise, old wolf named Akela led the pack.

Akela lay on his rock. Below him sat the other wolves. The wolf-cubs played in front of the rock. One by one they were looked over by the other wolves. Then it was Mowgli's turn.

A roar came from behind the rock.

"That cub is mine! Give him to me!"
It was Shere Khan.

Akela didn't twitch an ear.

"Who will help look after this cub?" he asked.

"I will help look after him," said Baloo, the sleepy, brown bear. He taught the Law of the Jungle to all the cubs.

"And I will help look after him too," said Bagheera the black panther.

Mowgli had a wonderful life. When he wasn't learning the Jungle Laws from Baloo, he sat out in the sun and slept. When he felt dirty or hot, he swam in the Jungle pools. When he wanted honey, he climbed trees to get it. He picked thorns from the paws of his friends.

He found that if he stared hard enough at any wolf, the wolf would have to look away. So he stared at the wolves for fun.

Mother Wolf told Mowgli that Shere Khan was not to be trusted. Bagheera told him that Shere Khan would kill him one day. But Mowgli laughed at this.

"Why should I be afraid?"

"Because Akela is getting old," said Bagheera. "The Pack will have a new leader. The young wolves believe Shere Khan can lead them. They do not think that a man-cub has a place in the Pack."

"I was born in the Jungle," said Mowgli. "I have obeyed its Laws. The wolves are my brothers."

"Look at me," said Bagheera.

Mowgli did, and the big panther was forced to turn his head away.

"They hate you because their eyes cannot meet yours. You must be ready. You must get some of the Red Flower."

Bagheera meant fire.

Mowgli ran to the nearest village. When he looked into a hut, he saw a boy put lumps of hot charcoal in a pot and carry it outside.

Mowgli snatched the pot from the boy and ran back to the Jungle. He met Bagheera on the way and held up the fire-pot.

"I am ready," he said.

That evening, Tabaqui the jackal came to Mowgli's cave and told him he was wanted at Akela's rock.

Shere Khan was there. It was time to choose a new leader. As Shere Khan began to speak, Mowgli sprang to his feet.

"Does Shere Khan lead the Pack?" he asked. "What has he to do with it?"

"Be quiet!" shouted some of the wolves.

Akela raised his old, tired head.

"I am no longer your leader. It is your right to kill me."

There was a hush. No one wanted to fight with Akela.

"It is the man-cub who should die!" roared Shere Khan as he looked at Mowgli. "Give him to me!"

"He hasn't broken any Jungle Law," said Akela.

"A man cannot be part of the Wolf Pack," said Shere Khan. "Give him to me."

"He is our brother," said Akela. "If you let him go, I promise I will die without a fight."

The wolves began to snarl and growl. "He is a man," they said.

Shere Khan's tail twitched.

"It is time to fight," whispered Bagheera to Mowgli.

Mowgli stood up with the fire-pot in his hand.

"I do not call you brothers any more," he said to the wolves.

He threw the fire-pot on the ground. Red-hot coals lit the grass. Mowgli put a branch into the fire until it crackled and burned. He held it above his head. The wolves were frightened.

"Save Akela from being killed," said Bagheera. "He is your friend."

Mowgli caught hold of Shere Khan by his chin.

"When I next come back to this rock, you will be dead. Now let Akela go free to live as he pleases."

Mowgli waved the burning branch at the wolves and Shere Khan. They ran off, howling with fear.

"Now I must go and live with the people in the village," said Mowgli to Bagheera. "First I must say goodbye to Mother Wolf."

"Come back soon," said Mother Wolf.

"Come back soon," said Father Wolf.

As dawn broke, Mowgli set off to the village.

Kaa's Hunting

All this happened in the days when Baloo was teaching Mowgli the Law of the Jungle. There was a lot to learn. Sometimes when Mowgli didn't get things right, Baloo would tap him with his big paw.

"But he is so small!" Bagheera would say.

"Is there anything too small to be killed?" Baloo would say. "When he knows all the Master Words of the Jungle, he will be able to call on any creature to protect him."

"I shall have a tribe of my own one day," said Mowgli. "I will lead them through the trees."

"You have been talking to the Monkey People," said Baloo. He was very angry.

"They were nice to me," said Mowgli. "They gave me nuts to eat and took me to the top of the trees. They said I will be their leader one day."

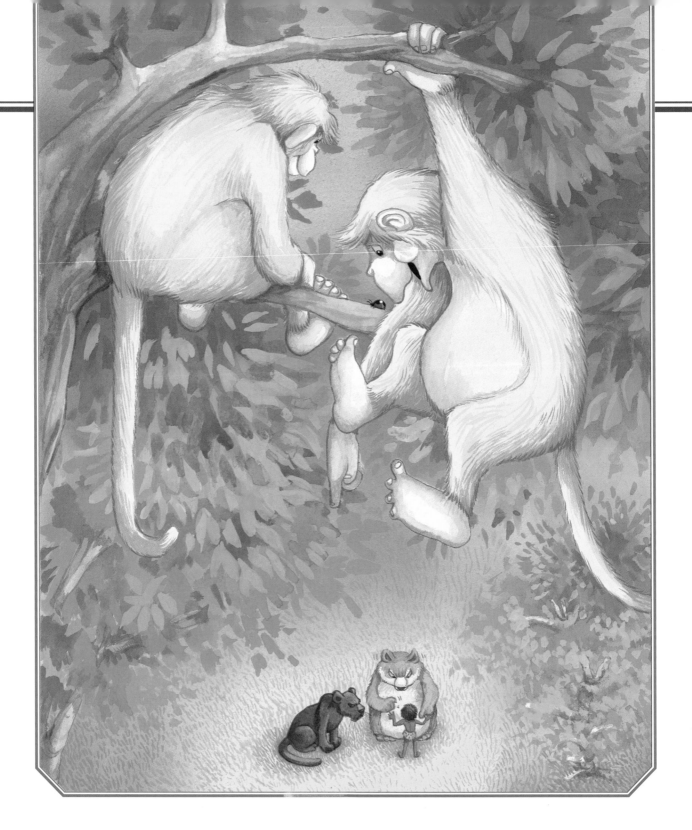

"Listen to me," said Baloo. "I have taught you the Law of the Jungle for all animals, except for the Monkey People. They have no law. Whenever they find a sick animal they tease it for fun. They will do anything to get themselves noticed."

Baloo did not know they were being watched by the monkeys. They followed the three friends through the Jungle until they settled down to sleep.

Suddenly Mowgli felt little hands on his legs and arms, and he was whisked into the trees. Baloo awoke with a cry and Bagheera jumped as high as he could. But it was too late. Two of the strongest monkeys had swung away with Mowgli through the tree tops.

Mowgli was afraid of being dropped. Then he grew angry.

He called out to a big bird in the sky. It was Chil the kite.

"Look where I am! Tell Baloo and Bagheera you have seen me," he shouted.

Chil nodded and rose up into the air, looking for Baloo and Bagheera.

Baloo and Bagheera were angry with themselves.

"We must make a plan," said Bagheera.

"The Monkey People are frightened of Kaa the Rock Snake," said Baloo. "He can climb as well as they can. He steals monkeys in the night. We must go and see Kaa."

They found Kaa stretched out in the afternoon
sun. He said he would help them rescue Mowgli.

"I have heard that the Monkey People have been
calling me names," said Kaa.

"They will say anything - even that you are afraid
of a goat!" said Baloo. He knew that this would
make Kaa angry.

"Which way did they go?" asked Kaa.
Suddenly Chil appeared above them.

"Look up! Look up!" he called. "The man-cub has been taken to the Monkey City."

It was growing dark and Mowgli was hungry. He knew he had to get back to his own part of the Jungle.

A cloud came over the moon. If it had been a bigger cloud, he would have tried to run away in the darkness.

Bagheera and Kaa were waiting for the same cloud to cover the moon.

"I will go to the west wall," whispered Kaa.

"I will go to the terrace," whispered Bagheera.

Mowgli heard the sound of Bagheera's light feet on the terrace. Suddenly howls of fright and anger could be heard as Bagheera struck out at the monkeys.

"There is only one! Kill him!" shouted the monkeys.

Mowgli was dragged away and pushed into a hole.

Bagheera was fighting for his life.

"Roll into the water tank, Bagheera!" shouted Mowgli.

Bagheera heard Mowgli's cry.

Then from the wall nearest the Jungle came a great roar. It was Baloo. He was joining the fight. Mowgli heard Bagheera splash into the water tank. The monkeys wouldn't follow him in there.

Kaa had worked his way over from the opposite wall. He was over thirty feet long. As soon as the monkeys saw him they ran.

"It is Kaa! Run! Run!"

The battle was won. Bagheera climbed from the water tank and Mowgli was pulled from the hole. He put his arms around Baloo and Bagheera.

Baloo and Bagheera were both bitten and sore.

"This happened because you played with the Monkey People," said Baloo.

"True," said Mowgli. "I am sorry."

The Law of the Jungle said Mowgli should be punished. Bagheera gave him six soft taps with his paw.

"Tiger! Tiger!"

Now we must return to the first tale. When Mowgli left after his fight with the wolves, he went to the village. The people came to the village gate to stare at him.

"He is a wolf-child. Now he has run away from the Jungle. We have nothing to fear from him."

Mowgli was taken to live with a woman named Messua.

One day, the head-man of the village told Mowgli he must go out and look after the buffaloes as they grazed.

Mowgli took the buffaloes to the edge of the plain where the river came out of the Jungle. There he met Grey Brother, one of Mother Wolf's four cubs when Mowgli was a baby.

"Have you any news of Shere Khan?" asked Mowgli.

"He's away hunting," said Grey Brother. "When he comes back he says he will kill you."

Grey Brother said he would let Mowgli know when Shere Khan was back.

The day Shere Khan returned, Grey Brother went to tell Mowgli that the tiger would wait for him outside the village gate.

Mowgli had a plan. He would use the buffalo herd to trap Shere Khan. As Mowgli would need some help, Grey Brother had brought Akela along with him.

Mowgli split the buffalo herd in two, with the bulls in one group and the cows in another. Shere Khan would be trapped between the two. The village boys thought Mowgli had gone mad, and they ran home.

Mowgli called out to Shere Khan.

"Who calls?" answered Shere Khan.

"It is Mowgli!"

Suddenly Akela howled at the top of his voice. The buffaloes began to gallop. Shere Khan heard the thunder of hooves. He looked for a way to escape but buffaloes charged at him from both directions.

Shere Khan was trampled beneath the buffaloes as they charged onto the plain.

When Mowgli began to remove Shere Khan's skin, he looked up to see Buldeo, who lived in the village.

Buldeo was angry. He said Mowgli must give the tiger skin to him.

"The skin is mine," said Mowgli.

When Mowgli took the buffaloes back to the village, the people were waiting for him at the gate.

"Go away, wolf-cub!" they shouted at him.

Mowgli did not understand.

"The wolves told me to go because I am a man. You tell me to go because I am a wolf!"

Messua ran up to Mowgli. "Buldeo says you are a wizard. I do not believe what they say about you. But you must go, or they will kill you."

Mowgli walked away with Grey Brother and Akela at his side. The moon was just going down when they arrived at Akela's rock.

Mother Wolf's eyes glowed when she saw the tiger skin.

"I said that one day you would kill Shere Khan," she said.

The wolves had been without a leader for a long time, but they still came when Akela called.

They saw Shere Khan's skin stretched out on the rock. They wanted someone to lead them again. But Bagheera said that could not be since they had chosen to be free.

From that day onwards, Mowgli and his four Grey Brothers hunted in the Jungle alone.